CHASE'S LOOSE TOOTH!

Adapted by Casey Neumann

Based on the episode "Pups Save a Toof" by Ursula Ziegler Sullivan

Illustrated by MJ Illustrations

A Random House PICTUREBACK® Book

Random House 🏠 New York

© 2018 Spin Master PAW Productions Inc. All rights reserved. Published in the United States by Random House Children's Books, a division of Penguin Random House LLC, 1745 Broadway, New York, NY 10019, and in Canada by Penguin Random House Canada Limited, Toronto. Pictureback, Random House, and the Random House colophon are registered trademarks of Penguin Random House LLC. PAW Patrol and all related titles, logos, and characters are trademarks of Spin Master Ltd. Nickelodeon, Nick Jr., and all related titles and logos are trademarks of Viacom International Inc.

rhcbooks.com

ISBN 978-1-5247-7271-0

MANUFACTURED IN CHINA

10 9 8 7 6 5 4 3 2 1

One sunny day, Chase, Marshall, Zuma, and Rubble were playing tug-of-war.

Suddenly, Chase lost his grip and fell backward with a thud. "Ouch!" he yelped. That was when he felt his tooth wiggle!

"What's wrong, Chase?" asked Marshall.

"My tooth ith looth!" Chase said.

"Loose teeth are awesome!" Zuma exclaimed. "When you put them under your pillow, the tooth fairy leaves you something great!"

But Chase wasn't convinced. He went to his doghouse to lie down.

Ryder joined the pups and peeked in on Chase.
"You should really have the dentist take a look at that," he said.
Chase was scared.
"There is nothing to be afraid of," Ryder reassured him.
"The dentist will make sure your teeth are healthy and strong."

Meanwhile, across town, Alex was playing in his tree house. It was time for his checkup at the dentist.

His grandpa, Mr. Porter, called for him to come down. But Alex didn't want to go.

Using the back of a hammer, Alex pried off the top few steps of his ladder.

"A broken ladder?" Mr. Porter said. "Guess I'll have to borrow one to help get you down."

"Yes!" Alex whispered to himself. "Now there won't be enough time to go to the dentist!"

Mr. Porter reached for his phone. "I bet the PAW Patrol can get you down in a jiffy," he said with a smile.

The pups and Ryder geared up and raced to the rescue. The PAW Patrol was on the roll!

The team arrived on the scene. Marshall backed up his fire truck and raised the ladder high. But Alex still refused to come down from the tree house.

"I'm scared of the dentist," he admitted.

"That's okay. Everyone is scared of something," Ryder explained.

"Not you and the PAW Patrol," Alex said.

That gave Ryder an idea.

"If I can get the PAW Patrol to do things they're scared of, will you go to the dentist?"

Alex agreed to Ryder's deal.

Ryder went first. He asked Mr. Porter to bring him the one thing that scared him the most—Brussels sprouts!

Mr. Porter handed Ryder a fresh Brussels sprout. Ryder chewed it up and swallowed it down.

"See? That wasn't so bad," he said to Alex.

"Rocky, what are you scared of?" Ryder asked.
"Um, well . . . uh . . . water," Rocky said. He asked
Marshall to spray him with his fire hose.

Marshall sprayed Rocky until he was soaking wet.
"Eww, now I'm gonna have that wet-pup smell!" Rocky whined.
Alex chuckled.

"And Rubble is afraid of spiders," Ryder said, picking up a spider with a stick. The spider traveled down a thread to Rubble's nose!

It sat there for a few seconds and then crawled away. Rubble was just fine!

"Marshall is scared of flying," Ryder said.
Skye locked Marshall into her harness and took off.
"This isn't so bad!" Marshall declared, dangling from Skye's chopper.
Suddenly, Skye spotted an eagle soaring toward them. "Look out!" she shouted. She made a sharp turn to avoid crashing into the bird. "I don't like eagles!"

"Wow, I didn't think the PAW Patrol was scared of anything," Alex said.

"Everyone is afraid of something, but sometimes you need to do things even though you're scared," Ryder said.

"If you can all be brave, so can I," Alex declared. "I'm going to the dentist!" He finally climbed down the ladder.

The pups cheered!

"Alex, could you help one last pup be brave?" Ryder asked.

Alex said he would.

"Chase is afraid of the dentist, too," said Ryder. "Maybe you can help him out."

If the police pup could see Alex being brave, then he could be brave!

"Sure I can!" Alex said.

Alex and Mr. Porter got a special escort from the
PAW Patrol to the dentist so they wouldn't be late.
No job was too big, no pup was too small!

When they reached the dentist's office, Chase and Alex bravely walked in together.

"Hooray!" cheered Ryder, Mr. Porter, and the other pups.

When their checkups were done, Alex and Chase told the others they had learned how to keep their teeth healthy and clean. "The dentist was super nice!" said Alex. "She gave me a sticker and a toothbrush!"

The dentist had pulled Chase's loose tooth. She said a new one would grow in its place.

"I'm going to put this tooth under my pillow tonight," said Chase, "and hopefully the tooth fairy will leave me an extra-special treat!"

The next morning, Chase woke up to find a shiny new bone from the tooth fairy. He took a big bite.

"Oh, no! I think I have another loose tooth!" he said.

All the pups laughed.